T0208688

The Sweet Life

by Elizabeth Counts

iUniverse, Inc.
New York   Bloomington

The Sweet Life

iUniverse books may be ordered through booksellers or by contacting:

iUniverse
1663 Liberty Drive
Bloomington, IN 47403
www.iuniverse.com
1-800-Authors (1-800-288-4677)

ISBN: 978-1-4401-1448-9 (pbk)
ISBN: 978-1-4401-1449-6 (ebk)

Printed in the United States of America

iUniverse rev. date: 5/28/2009

Contents

The Sweet Life

Your lips are like wine
Soft and sweet
Your body is like the ocean
Which flows through my blood
The caress of your skin
Brings beauty to life
And just to hold you
Comforts my soul
This feeling is blessed
Beyond my control
It's hard to describe
And hard to take hold
Treasure life's moments
And find the joy in life
For life passes so quickly
And true comfort is hard to find

Enjoy Life

Enjoy every moment of your life today
And your memories forever will be there to stay
But knowing life is never easy and we sometimes want to run and hide
Just remember *"I LOVE YOU"* and will also be by your
side

Living Alone

To live life alone
Or with another person, is left to be decided while I roam
True love is a miracle from God
And once it is found
Shall never be released

Only Time

Only time knows what the future may hold
And if only then can I wait what must be told
You've given me hope for a better tomorrow
And having you as a friend, I can no longer sorrow

I Love...

I Love...
- the sound of your voice as it grasps my soul
- the feel of your touch as you caress mine
- the warmth of your skin as we unite
- the movement of your breath as you breath
- the touch of your hand as it races my heart
- the thought of your heart entwined with mine
- AND................................**I LOVE YOU!**

Found You

When I found you my life became complete
You make me feel special
Knowing I have you brightens my everyday
And I just wanted to take this moment to say
HAPPY ANNIVERSARY MY LOVE!

Hope

Take every day of life with a hope of a better tomorrow
Seek relief in past memories while recalling the good times
   we shared
Just remember I am here if you ever need a friend

Live Once

For we only live once
And must enjoy life
Or we may die
Never knowing what we could have had

Joy

The joys of life have only begun
For you now will have a little one to play with and have
    fun
Nothing can ever surpass what you are about to see
Because this is "motherhood" and not make believe

Thank You

Thank you for the time you made me smile
It seemed like life was worth the while
Through thick and thin shallow or deep
I now will forever have something for keep
Though true friendship is hard to find
By remembering ours, I will always shine

Sharing

I want to love you without clutching
Appreciate you without judging
Join you without invading
Leave you without guilt
And help you without insulting
If I can have the same from you
Then we can truly meet and enrich each other

Softness

Mostly I want to give you softness
You seem on need of gently things right now
And room to play with no one keeping score
If I can bring you one thing new that catches your
     surprise and
saves your innocence, then I will bring it quickly
There are a few sounds I find as beautiful as my own
     piece of
mind and someone breathing softly next to me

Believe

Believe in yourself and you will see
That you can become what you want to be
Take pride in your work and approach each day with a
  smile
And you will see that life is worthwhile

I'm Sorry

I'm sorry for the hurt and pain that occurred between us
A simple matter of misunderstandings can harm a
 relationship
I cherish the moments we're together
And look forward to the anticipation of seeing you again
You've made me feel loved and womanly
We have so much to offer each other and shouldn't let it
 end

Every time

Every time you touch me my heart goes racing
The feeling you give me when we're together
Is beyond expression
I care for you deeply and completely
and will always be here
for you if you ever need me
Your breath is music to my ears
Don't forget what has evolved between us
And the love and passion we both feel
Let time take control and lead us together

The Times

The times we spend together are very special to me
Even though we are just beginning our relationship
I believe we feel a certain closeness
And just wanted to say....
I MISS YOU!

Sorry

Sorry for the hurt and pain you had to go through
Sometimes life is never easy
And we seek comfort from closest friends
Believe in yourself and things will get better
If you ever need a friend
I am here for listen

Longing

I long for the sight of your face
The feel of your skin
The sound of your voice
I wait patiently until I see you again
And hope that our passion for each other
Will keep us together

Everything

I want to release all my energy in you
I want to give you what you desire
Everything I am and do I want to do for you
Anytime you need me, I am here for you
Nothing in life is more important
Than having someone to love
And being loved in return

Open Your Heart

Open your heart and you shall see
That nothing is more important than love can be
For giving and receiving love plays only a part
But where it truly lies is within your heart
Though not knowing what the future holds
And what disasters my lie ahead
Keep faith in your love and what has been said
When the bondings complete and you feel you can't
   break
Believe in yourself because everything's at stake

Confusion

Confusion in life will always exist
Within life, love and relationships
Take one day at a time
And look forward to tomorrow
There's no need to dwell upon past pain and sorrow

Woman

A woman should take pride in who she is
And knowing its hers and not just his
Believe in your ambitions, goals and desires
And one day you'll realize that its all worthwhile

Trust

Trust in your heart and in your soul
And you will always know where you need to go
Destiny is one thing that we can't control
But we can help guide it the way it should flow

Heart to Heart

The beat of your heart is like the pedal of a flower
Soft and delicate with every hour
Hearts and flowers can be broken in time
But if you feed and nurture them, they will flourish
  forever

Desire

As you approach me, I see the flame and passion in your
  eyes
Time cannot be wasted and there shall be no goodbyes
Being near you my blood begins to boil
The beat of my heart grows fast
And just to be taken in your arms
Seems too short to last

Warmth

Warmth of the flame
Passion by desire
The love she has found
Is taking her higher

Knowing You

I would like us to get to know each other better
With the anticipation that one day we'll be together
The laughter we shared brightens my every day
And hope that you feel the same way

Family

Having a family is the greatest gift of life
Love for your child, husband or wife
Not just one person holds the key
But together they are a part

Laughter

You have given me laughter in a time of sorrow
You have given me hope in times of distress
You have given me strength in a time of fear
But most of all
You have given me YOU when I needed YOU most

GOD

God gave us feelings so that we may experience love
He gave us ambition so that we may rise above
He gave us caring so that we may help one another
He gave us sight so we may experience what beauty
    uncovers
He gave us faith to believe in him
He gave us confessions so that we may confess our sins
He gave us hope so that he will guide us through
And most of all he gave us each other
So that we may be true

Color My World

You color my world like the colors of a rainbow
You brighten my life like the light the stars show
Having you to love is all I ask for
I know I can't ask for anything more

Unite

When we're apart time goes slow
I wait patiently until I see you again
Wishing we could spend more time together
And hoping one day we can grow old
You have brought laughter into my life
And helped me see the good in things
I will never forget these you've given me
And hope one day we can unite

LOVE

Letting your true feelings show
Opening your arms in a time of need
Victory can be accomplished when two believe
Everything shall be out of love

Beyond

Beyond today is unknown
Only time knows what will be shown
What is beyond your grasp and out of sight
May soon appear in your light
Believe in the future and in all you do
And GOD will see you through

Where's the Passion?

Where's the passion that was once there
It's hard to reveal with so much fear
When love takes control of your mind
And there's complete joy that knows no time
Is healing a part of life or not a form in sight
Be positive with what lies ahead and be caring in all that
   is said
Does love conquer all, or do lies continue to fall
Give your time and all, and you shall not fall
Believe in your heart and you shall have a brand new start

Belong

My heart and soul belong to you
And will forever be true
My life seems empty without you by my side
And my heart beats on, but only in strides
I am here for you whenever you need
Life is too short and reaps only one seed
Did you and I meet for a reason
Or was it only for fun
Because the day we met up rose the sun

GOD Teaches

God teaches us all to trust and not fall
But when one finds true love, we stand tall
I believe in true love that comes once on a lifetime
And finding ours, I will forever shine
I believe in Soul Mates that if found lasts forever
With ups and downs we can master any kind of weather
Why do things happen like they do
To teach us a lesson or learn to be true

At First Sight

When I saw you I couldn't believe my eyes
I had to get to know you before the next sunrise
You captured my eyes and made my heart race
Nothing was more important than being at that place
My heart was racing and my nerves were aflame
I was so confused and I had no one to blame
Does this mean anything and can life go on
My heart is alive just like a song
Can love always bloom when you meet someone new
For GOD gives you hope in believing its true

Always Believe

The greatest gifts of life, is to give and receive love
Cherish what life brings and you can rise above
Enjoy the gift of life because there is only one
Make the best of things and always have fun
So back to true love, 'O what can it be?
Is it simply a feeling that we can not see
Or is it an action that we must perform
Or is it a gift to give engraved when we are born
Whatever it may be, we are here to receive
And have faith in love and ALWAYS BELIEVE!

Loving Kindness

I wish to THANK YOU for being you
And all the funny things you do
Your sense of humor and zest for life
You are one of the few
You bring laughter to life
And always smile
Even when life gets stressful all the while

My Dear

My heart and soul belong to you
And will forever be true

My life seems empty
Without you by my side
And my heart beats on
But only in strides

I am here for you
Whenever you need
Life is too short
And reaps only 1 seed

Did you and I meet for a reason
Or was it only for fun
Because the day we meet
Up rose the sun

God teaches us all
To trust and not fall
But when one finds true love
We stand tall

I believe in true love
That comes once in a lifetime
And in finding our
I will forever shine

I believe in Soul Mates
That if found last forever
With ups and downs
We can master any kind of weather

Why do things happen like they do
To teach us a leason or learn to be true!

Greatest Gift

One of the greatest gifts of life
Is to fall in love
For this we cannot achieve
But only comes from heaven above

God takes care of us
And supplies us with what we need

So if you feel lost and alone
Keep your faith
And you'll never be far from home

Time Apart

The times were apart
Seems to long to endure
For the comfort I feel when I'm with you
Seems I only need you more

You have brighten my days
When all seemed dazed
To have someone like you
Sets my heart ablaze

You are near to my heart
More than words can say
For time only knows
Which is our way

Heart to Heart

The sound of your voice
Makes my heart rejoice
Someone who can give
Without ever wondering why
And who is not afraid to show himself
Or even cry
Believe that there is someone
Who wants to be near
For nothing is more detrimental
Then our own fear
Life is to short and precious
Then to go on alone
For having someone to love
Makes it feel like home
Take each day as it comes
And be happy and free
Because we only live once
And God controls our destiny
We are put throught test after test
And can only do our very best

Your Eyes

Your eyes are the window to your soul
So bright and so clear

Your heart is the key
That unlocks all your fear

Your mind is stronger
And remembers it all

And your body is alive
And will not fall

Miles Apart

We're miles apart
And the future seems unsure
And one thing is true
Is that our life is pure

Can true love really be
To find someone so dear
And knowing that nothing can
Stand in our way
And we have nothing to fear

Soul Mates

When you fall in love
And always seem to be in tears
Is it because you fell to hard
And now would rather die?

Do we ruin our lives
And we can not see
And in the end
We ask God to set us free!

Author Biography

My inspirations to write this book came from my mother, Jacqueline Lauck, who was also teacher and writer. The writings in this poem are based on real life experiences and feelings.

GOD has blessed me with a beautiful son whom I will cherish when I'm alive and deceased. I pray he has a fullfiling, rewarding, prosperious and loving life.

GOD has given us his loving kindness and I am bless to be given the talent of writing and dedicate this book to my mother, Jacqueline Lauck, my father, Glen Counts who are both deceased and the joy in my life; my son, George Dasco.